A Cardboard
CHRISTMAS

OTHER CHRISTMAS BOOKLETS
BY MICHELE ASHMAN BELL:

A Candle in the Window

A Cardboard CHRISTMAS

MICHELE ASHMAN BELL

Covenant Communications, Inc.

I'm hungry, Jimmy," eight-year-old Charlie complained to his older brother.

"I'm hungry, too," little Lizzie echoed. She was five but was sickly small for her age.

"It's almost done," Jimmy said as he poured the packet of powdered cheese on the cooked elbow macaroni. They didn't have butter or milk for the macaroni and cheese. Water would have to do.

Dumping a spoonful for each of them, Jimmy handed his younger brother and sister their plates and ate his share out of the pan.

"Where's Mommy?" Lizzie asked, her mouth full of noodles.

"She's working two shifts. She won't be home till late," Jimmy told her.

"Will she be home in the morning before you leave for school?" Lizzie asked. She hated it when she was left alone while her brothers were at school and her mom was at the diner.

"She'll be home," Jimmy told him. "Now eat, it's time for bed." It was his job to tend the kids after school until his mom got home from work. But sometimes she picked up extra hours to make some extra money. It was hard for him to keep up with his homework and keep his siblings out of trouble, but he'd worked hard to get into Mr. Payne's advanced sixth grade math class, and he didn't want to get sent back to the regular class just because he couldn't handle the work.

"It's cold in here," Lizzie said with a shiver.

"The house is always cold," Jimmy told her. They kept the thermostat low so they wouldn't run up a large heating bill. But it seemed cold even for their house. He checked the thermostat, which registered fifty-nine. When he bumped up the temperature, it didn't click on.

"I think the pilot light's out," he said.

"Can you light it?" Charlie asked, scraping the last bite of pasta from his plate.

"I watched Mom do it one time, but I can't remember what she did," he told them.

"We'll freeze tonight if we don't get it turned on," Charlie pressed.

Jimmy thought for a moment, looking at his tiny sister shivering in a thin, oversized T-shirt. "I'll be right back. You guys brush your teeth and get ready for bed." Jimmy grabbed his coat and headed out the door.

He walked next door to Mr. Meyers's house and stood several minutes on the man's porch before he found the nerve to knock. But Jimmy was desperate, and the man's light was still on.

After knocking, Jimmy shifted his weight from foot to foot to keep moving, trying to stay warm. The cold nipped at his earlobes, making them throb in the frigid evening air.

A shuffling of feet behind the door brought him to attention. He also thought he heard mumbling—or maybe it was more like grumbling.

The door jerked open, and the grouchy old man with a ragged beard and bushy gray hair that stuck out in tufts all over his head glared down at Jimmy. "What do you want?" he snarled.

Jimmy shrank back, ready to run. Then he thought of Lizzie. She was too tiny and weak to handle the cold. They had to get the furnace back on again. *Do it for Lizzie and Charlie,* he told himself.

"Mr. Meyers," he said haltingly.

"Speak up, boy!" the man snapped.

"Our furnace," Jimmy said louder. "It's gone out."

The man's eyebrows knitted together. "What do you want me to do about it, boy?"

"My mom's at work. Could you . . ." Jimmy swallowed. "Do you think you . . ." He shut his eyes and took a deep breath. "Could you light it for us?"

Mr. Meyers's eyes grew round, as if he couldn't believe the boy was requesting such an inconvenient favor.

Jimmy felt that his knees might buckle as a wave of nausea washed over him. He'd never even said two words to this man. He'd always been warned by his mother not to bother Mr. Meyers. She hadn't needed to worry—Jimmy had never had any intention of talking to the man. Not until now.

Digging deep for courage, Jimmy looked up into the man's pinched, wrinkled face expecting a negative answer.

With a huff of annoyance, Mr. Meyers finally said, "Oh, all right." He turned and reached for his coat and then grabbed a long-nosed lighter off his mantle as he mumbled, "Guess it doesn't matter that I was on my way to bed. Folks don't show respect for the elderly anymore."

Jimmy tried to ignore the man's comments. Hurrying ahead of Mr. Meyers, Jimmy led the way to the side door of his house that went into the kitchen.

There, Charlie and Lizzie were huddled around a candle to keep warm, holding their palms as close to the flame as they dared.

"Where'd you go?" Charlie asked. "I thought maybe you went to get Prune Face." A sudden look of horror struck his expression when Mr. Meyers walked in behind Jimmy.

Mr. Meyers glared at the young boy, then his gaze slipped over to tiny Lizzie warming her hands. A look of fear crossed her eyes, and she immediately scooted next to Charlie.

Studying the two smaller children a minute longer, Mr. Meyers then glanced around the messy kitchen where dirty dishes overflowed in the sink and the counter was piled with clutter.

"Where's your mother?" he growled with impatience.

"She's at work," Jimmy said.

"Doesn't anyone ever clean up around here?"

Jimmy glanced around at the kitchen, then shrugged. "Sometimes."

"You kids could clean up after yourselves," he said gruffly, shaking his head. "Where's the furnace?"

Jimmy led him down the hallway and opened the door to where the furnace was.

"Got a flashlight?" he asked.

Jimmy knew they had one, but he didn't know if the batteries worked. With the other kids helping, he scoured the house looking for a flashlight but couldn't find one.

"Run over to my house," Mr. Meyers said, his voice tight with his growing impatience. "Right inside the door is a flashlight on the coatrack. Bring it to me."

Jimmy ran as quickly as he could. Snatching the flashlight, he raced back to his house, where he found Charlie and Lizzie in the hallway with Mr. Meyers.

Lizzie was telling the old man that she'd seen Santa Claus earlier that day. It was obvious that Mr. Meyers didn't want to hear about it, but once Lizzie got going on something, she didn't stop until she was done. "He gave me a candy cane and a coloring book," she said excitedly, "except I don't have any crayons. But he said maybe he would bring me some at Christmas. I said all I want is a new dress. I have to wear Charlie and Jimmy's old clothes. So I'm asking Santa for a red, velvet dress. With ruffles and lace and a bow. A princess dress."

"You're not going to get one," Charlie told her. "Santa's not bringing us nothin'," he said. "He never does."

Lizzie's expression fell, and her bottom lip curled.

"Come on, you guys." Jimmy handed Mr. Meyers the flashlight and pulled his brother and sister away. "Go get the blanket on Mommy's bed and sit on the couch."

Mr. Meyers flashed the light on the furnace and opened the cover. "Here." Mr. Meyers thrust the flashlight toward Jimmy. "Hold this."

The man turned some knobs and flicked the lighter and held it at the bottom of the furnace for a minute. The pilot light flared, and the furnace kicked on.

Making a few more adjustments, Mr. Meyers then replaced the cover.

"Tell your mom the filters need to be changed."

Jimmy nodded and handed the man his flashlight.

"It should warm up soon," he said.

Mr. Meyers walked toward the kitchen door, pausing by the front room to see Charlie and Lizzie huddled together under a thin, threadbare blanket. A wooden chair sat in one corner with a small television sitting on top of it, out of which poked a wire hanger used for an antenna.

A pair of drapes barely hung on their rod, held in place only by three or four hooks.

Just as he turned to leave, Lizzie called out, "Thank you for making us warm again. Merry Christmas, Mr. Meyers."

"Lizzie, shh." Charlie elbowed her beneath the blanket.

"Ow, Charlie! That hurt," she whimpered.

Mr. Meyers took one last look, shook his head, and left without saying another word.

* * *

As bad as Jimmy hated the cold and the snow, it provided him with an opportunity to earn money. Carrying a used snow shovel that was bent and crooked, Jimmy went out after each snowstorm, door to door, offering to shovel walks for money.

Most people were generous, if they hadn't already cleared their walks with a snow blower. Jimmy was able to earn a few dollars each time he went out. He knew he couldn't rely on Santa or anyone else to bring gifts for his family for Christmas, but he could rely on himself.

Sometimes, when he walked past Mr. Meyers's house, he saw the old man looking at him through the window. Jimmy wondered why the man was so grouchy. The man had the nicest home on the street and drove the nicest car too. He could probably have anything he wanted, but he just didn't seem happy. It didn't make sense to Jimmy.

One Saturday morning, Jimmy woke up to find that three inches of snow had fallen through the night. Wishing he could sleep in, but knowing that wasn't a luxury he could afford, he quickly dressed and headed outside to get to people's driveways before anyone else did.

When he raced through the kitchen, Charlie and Lizzie were already up and eating a bag of microwave popcorn for breakfast. Their mother hadn't gotten in until three o'clock in the morning, so she was still asleep. Jimmy told them to wash the dishes in the sink and pick up the mess in the living room.

Their complaints landed on deaf ears as he walked out into the icy morning air. Dragging his shovel behind him, Jimmy headed down the street, hoping to have some luck getting snow-shoveling jobs. Christmas wasn't too far away, and he didn't have much money saved.

Three driveways later, Jimmy, half-frozen and dead tired, headed home. By now it was midmorning and nearly everyone had cleaned off their walks. Everyone but Jimmy's family and Mr. Meyers.

Jimmy walked past the house, glancing sideways to see if by chance Mr. Meyers was looking out the window. The old man wasn't there.

He remembered how Mr. Meyers had come over and lit their pilot light, and a thought suddenly struck him. Even though he was tired and cold, he stopped and began shoveling the sidewalk in front of Mr. Meyers's house and then worked his way up the driveway until it was clear of snow.

Later that day Jimmy happened to glance up and notice a delivery truck pull up in front of Mr. Meyers's house. All three children watched as deliverymen wheeled a new, large-screen television up to his house.

"Wish we had a TV like that," Lizzie said.

"Wish we had a TV with more than three channels that worked," Charlie replied.

"At least we have a TV," Jimmy said. "Come on. Mom will be home from work early. Let's have dinner ready. We can make grilled cheese sandwiches."

"We have cheese?" Charlie asked excitedly.

Lizzie pulled a face at the mention of the food.

"Lizzie, what's wrong?" Jimmy asked.

She shrugged. "I want some soup."

Jimmy worried about his little sister. She didn't look right—her eyes, her coloring, something, he wasn't sure what.

A while later, their mother walked through the door. "Hi, kids," she said as she plopped her purse and coat onto the counter. The children were seated around the kitchen table, eating dinner. It took all the strength she had to give them each a hug and a kiss. "Sorry I'm late. Luis our dishwasher was late, so I volunteered to stay after and wash dishes until he showed up."

"We made dinner," Jimmy said proudly, holding up a grilled cheese sandwich for his mother. "And soup."

Laura gave her oldest son a smile. "It looks great, sweetie. Why don't you save that for me? I need to go lie down for a little while. I'm exhausted."

The three children looked up at her, their faces smudged and lacking the exuberance of childhood. They carried far too many burdens for children so young. She hated how much she had to leave them and how ragged and starved they were. But it was all she could do to keep a roof over their heads and something in their stomachs. She worked as long and as hard as she was physically able to, but it still just wasn't enough.

"After my nap, we'll get the Christmas decorations out," she told them.

All three of the kids cheered at her suggestion.

"Give me a half an hour or so," she said, tousling the hair on Charlie's head. Then she looked at her daughter more closely. "Lizzie, sweetie, you don't look well. Are you sick?"

"I'm okay, Mommy," she said, covering her mouth as she coughed.

"Why don't you come and take a nap with me? You look like you could use some sleep."

Lizzie pushed her barely eaten bowl of soup away and got up from the table. Putting her tiny hand in her mother's, they left the room.

Charlie waited until they were gone, then said, "I know where the decorations are. We could get them out right now and surprise Mom and Lizzie."

Jimmy thought about it for a moment. Their mom was so tired, she'd probably appreciate it if they did pull out the decorations.

"Okay," Jimmy said, "let's put the dishes in the sink first. And save that soup for Lizzie. She only had a few bites."

The two boys cleaned off the table and were soon looking for the box of decorations in the storage room. With their arms loaded, they made a pile in the front room and began going through the decorations. They found strands of lights, candles, stockings for the mantel, and several handmade decorations for the walls.

"Look," Jimmy said, reaching for a shoebox, "here's the nativity set."

He lifted the box carefully, knowing that it wasn't just precious because it was a porcelain set of Mary, Joseph, and baby Jesus in a manger, but because it was the last gift their father had given to their mother before he died in a car accident two years ago.

"Let's put it on the windowsill like we did last year," Charlie suggested.

They carefully placed the pieces of the nativity on the windowsill, where the silver glow of the streetlight illuminated the figurines.

"Oh, pretty!" Lizzie's voice came from edge of the room. "You put up the nativity set."

"We wanted to surprise Mom," Jimmy explained to her.

Lizzie hurried across the room to see the set, but she tripped on the jumble of boxes and decorations strewn about the floor. She reached out to catch herself, but bumped against the windowsill. The three children watched as the pieces of the nativity crashed to the floor as if in slow motion and broke into dozens of pieces.

Horror struck their hearts. Jimmy bent down and picked up his sister, who'd collapsed in tears. "Don't cry, Lizzie," he told her.

"That was Mommy's favorite thing in the whole world. And I broke it," she sobbed.

Jimmy continued to hold her while she wept and apologized. Finally, she cried herself to sleep. He took her to her bed and covered her with a blanket.

"What are we going to do?" Charlie asked his older brother when he returned.

Jimmy had wondered the same thing. He had a few dollars saved, and he was hoping to make even more money before Christmas. Maybe if he worked really hard, he could come up with enough money to buy his mom another nativity set.

"Don't tell Mom yet," he told his little brother. "Let's pick up the pieces and hide the box so she doesn't find it like this."

They went to their bedroom and found a spot in the back of their closet where they covered the box with an old sleeping bag and some of their toys.

On their way back to the living room to finish sorting the decorations, Jimmy stopped outside his mother's bedroom door. He heard a noise. A soft, sad noise.

The sound of his mother crying nearly broke Jimmy's heart. For a moment, he wondered if she knew about the nativity set, but he knew that wasn't it. Losing their father had been hard for his mom. She worked long hours to make enough money for them to live, but she just couldn't seem to make ends meet. But it wasn't just the hard work that was difficult. There was an emptiness in their home. Nothing filled up the hole.

Especially at Christmas.

Jimmy decided to try to do even more to help out his mom. Maybe he could find another job or try and do snow removal on the next street over. He decided to do whatever it took to buy his mom the nativity set. He just had to.

* * *

The next night, the phone rang just as Jimmy got the two younger children in bed. They decided to sleep together in Charlie's bed because it got so cold in Lizzie's room and she had a hard time staying warm. She still didn't feel well and hadn't eaten much of her dinner. Her cough was becoming croupy and painful.

"Hi, sweetie," his mom said when he answered the phone.

Jimmy immediately noticed concern in his mom's voice.

"Honey, I'm going to be a little late. My car broke down, and I had to have it towed to a garage. They have to replace the starter engine."

Jimmy didn't know exactly what a starter engine was, but it seemed like every time the car needed to be repaired, it cost more money than they had.

"I'll hurry home as soon as I can," she told him.

Jimmy told his mother good-bye and wondered why so many bad things kept happening to their family. Wasn't it enough that they barely had enough food to eat, that they wore clothes that didn't fit them right, and that their house was so cold they could see their breath in the morning?

* * *

The next morning, as Jimmy got himself and Charlie ready for school, he found his mom sitting at the kitchen table, resting her head in her hands. She looked like she hadn't slept all night.

"Hurry, Charlie," Jimmy hollered behind him. "We're going to miss the bus."

"Sweetie, come here," Jimmy's mom said.

He walked over to the table and looked into his mother's red-rimmed eyes.

"On your way home from school, I want you to take this money." She handed him a few dollars. "Buy some bread and milk. If there's any left over, buy some little candies for you and your brother and sister for Christmas. Okay?" She tried to give her son a smile, but her bottom lip trembled.

"Is Lizzie going to be okay?" Jimmy asked, putting the money in the zippered pouch of his backpack.

"She coughed all night," his mother answered. "I don't think she's getting any better. I don't have to go in to work until three.

Charlie will get home before I have to leave, but hurry home as soon as you can. Okay?"

"I will," he said, looping his arms through the straps of his pack.

Charlie came into the room, wearing an old sweatshirt and a pair of Jimmy's pants that were three sizes too big for him. He had a belt cinching them tightly around his waist.

A honk from the bus sent the two boys running, and for a moment, their only concern was getting to the bus before it left them. It was a long, cold walk to school.

That night after their dinner of peanut butter and jelly sandwiches, Charlie and Jimmy did their homework at the kitchen table while Lizzie laid on the couch watching a program on TV.

"Jimmy," she called from the couch. "Jimmy?"

He hurried in to see what his sister needed.

"What's wrong?" he asked, looking at her tiny body huddled under a blanket on the worn, sagging couch.

"Where's our Christmas tree?" she asked.

"We don't have one yet," he answered, knowing that most likely they wouldn't have one this year. There was no way they could afford it.

"But we need to put up a tree, or Santa won't come," she said with a sense of urgency, which caused her to begin coughing. Finally, she settled down, whimpering into her pillow.

Jimmy reached out and stroked her matted hair. He looked around the room and saw the pile of lights in the corner, waiting for a tree. Then he saw the empty coatrack near the door and got an idea.

"Lizzie, what if we hang the lights on the coatrack? They'll still look pretty turned on, until we get the tree."

"Can we, Jimmy?" She showed a spark of enthusiasm.

With Charlie's help, they untangled the strands of lights and draped them over the coatrack.

"Do you want to plug them in?" Jimmy asked Lizzie.

She nodded her head and pushed herself to her feet. Jimmy helped her to the wall where she took the plug and placed it in the socket.

The lights flashed on brightly, then there was a loud *zap!* All the lights in the house went black.

Lizzie immediately started crying.

"What do we do now?" Charlie asked.

Jimmy thought for a minute, wishing he knew. It was only seven o'clock at night. They couldn't spend the next three hours in the dark.

"Charlie." He hated the mere thought of what he was about to say. "You need to go over to Mr. Meyers's house and ask him to come over."

"Mr. Meyers's house? No way. I'm not going over there."

Lizzie whimpered again and clung to her oldest brother.

"You have to. He'll know what to do."

Stomping his feet loudly in his holey shoes, Charlie slammed the door behind him as he walked next door.

Lizzie finally settled down just as Jimmy heard footsteps coming up the walk. Charlie burst through the door, Mr. Meyers behind him.

"Jimmy, you should see Mr. Meyers's TV set," Charlie blurted out. "It's huge! The people on the screen are as big as real life."

Jumping to his feet, Jimmy didn't even answer his brother, but he told Mr. Meyers what happened. The last thing he wanted to do was waste the man's time.

"Sounds like you blew a fuse," the old man said. "Where's your fuse box?"

It took some searching, but they soon found the box, and after flipping several switches, the lights turned on.

Jimmy released a sigh of relief.

Mr. Meyers showed him how to flip the switches, just in case it happened again.

"Thanks, Mr. Meyers," Jimmy told the man. "Sorry we bothered you again."

The old man made his way to the door, stopping for a moment to see Charlie with some duct tape and his shoes on the table.

"Charlie, what are you doing?" Jimmy questioned.

"Covering the holes with tape so my feet don't get cold. The snow keeps coming inside."

Mr. Meyers looked at the boy at the table, then at Jimmy.

"Mr. Meyers," Lizzie called from the couch, "look at our lights." The Christmas lights shone brightly from the coatrack. "Aren't they pretty?"

Mr. Meyers nodded. "Yes, they are."

Lizzie started hacking again and pulled the blanket over her head as she coughed.

Mr. Meyers's brow narrowed, then he turned and headed for the door.

"Come here, boy," he signaled to Jimmy.

Jimmy wondered what he wanted.

"You don't have a father, do you?" he asked.

"He died two years ago."

"Don't you have any grandparents or relatives?" he asked.

"We have an uncle in Florida, but I've never met him," Jimmy answered.

Mr. Meyers nodded thoughtfully. He looked at Lizzie and Charlie one last time, sighed, and shook his head. "You kids stay warm," he said, then opened the door and left.

* * *

Jimmy was ecstatic. His friend at school needed help with his paper route while he was gone for Christmas break, which meant Jimmy could make some extra money. It also meant getting up at five in the morning, going over to his friend's house, and getting the papers and delivering them, but he was willing to do it.

He worked harder than he ever had, delivering papers and shoveling walks, and within a week's time, he finally had enough money to buy his mom the nativity set. He'd found it at the gift shop on the corner downtown. It was just like the one his father had given her, the statues' faces painted in delicate colors, almost lifelike.

Before he bought the set, Jimmy first talked to Charlie and Lizzie, telling them that the nativity set would take all the money he had, which meant they wouldn't be getting much for Christmas. But, just like he'd expected, neither of them cared. They were more excited to replace the broken nativity set than to get anything for themselves.

As soon as he brought the set home, the three children set it up on the windowsill in their living room. On a piece of brown felt, Jimmy set the figure of Joseph. Charlie placed the figure of Mary kneeling beside it. And between them, Lizzie placed the manger with the tiny baby Jesus in it.

"There," Lizzie said with satisfaction. "Now it feels like Christmas."

Using pieces of cardboard from the lids of some old shoe-boxes, the three children cut out stars, and with glue and glitter, they decorated the stars to hang in the window over the nativity scene.

After they were done, Lizzie sat for a long time looking up at the stars. Then, out of the blue she said, "Do you think Jesus can see us?"

Jimmy shrugged. He wasn't sure about anything like that anymore. Because if Jesus could see them, why would He let so many bad things happen to them?

"Sure He can," Charlie answered matter-of-factly. "He sees everything we do."

"Then He knows that we're thinking about Him?" she asked.

"He knows everything we think," Charlie told her.

"And Daddy?" she asked. "Does Daddy see us and know that we think about him?"

"Of course, Lizzie. Don't be stupid."

Jimmy was amazed at Charlie's absolute confidence in his answers.

That was all Lizzie needed to hear. She believed her brother without question and was satisfied.

But Jimmy wasn't. He certainly didn't want to make Heavenly Father mad at him, but he couldn't help wondering why everything had to be so hard. Sometimes, when he thought about it, he felt angry inside. Angry and sad.

After Jimmy finished his homework, he told Charlie and Lizzie it was time for bed. Charlie jumped up and turned off the TV, but Lizzie remained still and motionless on the couch.

"Lizzie's asleep," Charlie told his brother.

"I'll carry her into bed, you go turn down the covers," Jimmy told his brother. But when he picked up his little sister, he realized she wasn't just asleep. She was burning up with fever.

Panic struck his heart.

"Lizzie," he said, patting her hand. "Lizzie, wake up."

She mumbled something groggily but didn't seem to possess the strength to speak or open her eyes.

"Lizzie!" he cried.

Charlie rushed to her side and saw immediately what was going on.

"We have to call Mom," he said. "Lizzie's gonna die!"

"She's not gonna die," Jimmy snapped. But inside he'd had the same thoughts.

Fifteen long, frightening minutes later, their mother rushed through the door.

She felt Lizzie's forehead and tried desperately to rouse her daughter. Lizzie lay limp and weak, like a rag doll.

"We need to get her to the hospital," Laura cried.

Wrapping Lizzie in a blanket, they all rushed to the car.

"Pray, boys," Laura said through tears of worry and fear. "Pray for your sister."

* * *

The man at the register greeted Jimmy with a confused expression as Jimmy placed the nativity set with the receipt on the counter.

"I need to return this, please," Jimmy said.

"Didn't your mother like it?" the man asked.

"She didn't see it," Jimmy said. "I just can't get it right now."

The man nodded his head but didn't press further. "Do you want me to hold it for you for a few days?"

Jimmy wanted more than ever to have the man keep the nativity set for him, but he knew nothing would be different in two days. Lizzie would still be sick, and they would still need money to pay for the doctor.

Feeling someone behind him, Jimmy turned around and glanced up. His eyes grew wide. Mr. Meyers!

The man looked down at him with cold, gray eyes.

"Here you go, son," the man at the register said. "Here's your money. I'll hang onto that set for you, just in case something changes. Okay?"

Jimmy took the money and shoved it into his coat pocket. "Okay," he mumbled, tripping over his feet as he hurried from the store.

Bursting through the kitchen door, Jimmy startled Charlie.

"Where's Mom?" Jimmy asked.

"She's at the hospital. They're letting Lizzie come home tomorrow," Charlie told him.

Tomorrow was Christmas Eve. Jimmy was grateful that Lizzie could at least be home for Christmas so that they could all be together.

He went into his mother's room to leave the money on her pillow, but when he reached into his pocket to get it, it was gone.

He searched every pocket in his clothes three or four times.

Rushing outside, he began retracing his steps. The money must've fallen out when he pulled his glove out of his pocket. As fast as he could, he raced to the gift shop, scanning every inch of his path for the wad of bills from his pocket.

Angry tears stung his eyes. Why did everything go wrong? Couldn't Heavenly Father help them just this once?

"We need that money," he pleaded outloud. "Please," he begged the heavens, "help me find that money."

But it was nowhere to be found. That money wouldn't make much difference to someone else, but it meant the world to Jimmy and his family.

Charlie had gone to bed when Jimmy got home. Jimmy sat in the dark, looking out at the snow that had begun to fall.

He looked up at the stars hanging in the window. There was the star that represented the star of Bethlehem, the star that led the wise men and shepherds to the Savior. The star that guided them and gave them hope of the birth of the Messiah.

Jimmy looked at the stars but didn't feel any hope. Only despair. They didn't even have enough money for food, let alone any Christmas presents. And poor little Lizzie deserved something for Christmas. And what about their mother? She wouldn't have her treasured nativity set.

The next morning was Christmas Eve. Jimmy left Charlie home watching cartoons while he looked for a driveway that hadn't yet been shoveled. He managed to pick up a few dollars clearing a sidewalk for a woman, but the previous night's snow had already melted.

Dragging his shovel home behind him, Jimmy thought about Lizzie coming home that day. He wished more than anything that they could do something to make Christmas happy.

When he got to Mr. Meyers's house, he noticed the big cardboard box stacked next to the garbage cans, and a thought suddenly struck him.

He didn't even ask permission to take the box, figuring Mr. Meyers probably wouldn't care if Jimmy took something out of his garbage.

Banging through the door, Jimmy called for Charlie.

"What are you doing with that?" Charlie asked when he saw the big box.

"We're going to make a Christmas tree," he said.

Charlie burst out laughing. "A Christmas tree? Out of cardboard?"

"It's all we've got. Come on. Let's hurry before Lizzie gets home."

They managed to cut the shape of a five-foot Christmas tree out of the box. Using the last of a stubby green crayon they found at the bottom of Charlie's backpack, they colored as much of the cardboard as they could, then, with a screwdriver, they began poking holes through the cardboard. Taking the strand of Christmas lights, they poked the bulbs through the holes. They added some of the glittering stars that were hanging from the window, then propped the tree up in the corner. Crossing their fingers they plugged in the lights. The tree looked even more beautiful than they'd hoped.

"She's going to love it," Charlie said.

Jimmy nodded. It wasn't the real thing, but it was better than nothing.

"Grab your coat. We have to run to the store," Jimmy told his brother. He only had a few dollars, but they could at least buy some candy for Lizzie's Christmas sock.

Running to the neighborhood grocery store, they hurried in and purchased some candy canes, a chocolate Santa, and, to their delight, they had enough for a box of crayons.

Bursting with excitement, they ran home, anxious to hide the gifts before Lizzie got home.

Just as they got the house straightened and everything ready, their mother's car pulled up the driveway. Running outside, Jimmy and Charlie greeted their little sister with giant hugs. There was color in her cheeks and a smile on her face.

"Guess who I saw at the hospital before I left today?" she said.

They both shrugged.

"Santa Claus!" she said excitedly. "He gave me a new pencil and a notebook."

"That's great, Lizzie," Jimmy said.

"We have a surprise for you," Charlie told her.

"A surprise?" her eyes sparkled. "For me?"

"Boys?" their mother said, her eyes searching their faces. "What kind of surprise? Lizzie can't get too worked up. She still needs to take it easy until she's all the way better."

"You'll see," Jimmy said.

Keeping her eyes closed, Lizzie wiggled in her mother's arms, anxious to see what her surprise was.

"Okay," Jimmy said, waiting for Charlie to plug in the lights, "Open your eyes."

Slowly, Lizzie opened her eyes and saw the bright and shining cardboard Christmas tree in the corner of the room. She gasped, putting one of her tiny hands over her mouth. "Wow!" she said breathlessly.

With her mother's help, she walked over to the tree, noticing the stars and gently touching the lights. "It's the most beautiful thing I've ever seen."

Jimmy and Charlie smiled at each other. Making Lizzie happy made them both feel extra warm inside.

"Boys," their mom said, "this is really wonderful what you've done. Thank you." She gave each of her son's a giant hug. "I'm sorry that we don't have any presents to put under this lovely tree. Between the car and doctor bills—"

"It's okay, Mom," Jimmy said. "We're together. That's the best thing."

Tears brimmed in her eyes as she looked at her oldest child. "You're right. That is the best thing."

She looked around the room. "You've done such a great job decorating for Christmas." Then she stopped and searched again. Jimmy's heart sank. He knew that she'd realized what was missing.

"I don't see the nativity set. Did you forget to put it out?" she asked.

Jimmy didn't know whether to lie and tell her they couldn't find it, or tell her the truth and ruin her Christmas.

He didn't have time to answer. A knock came at the door, causing all of them to look at each other with wonder.

"Jimmy, would you answer it?" his mother requested.

Hurrying to the door, Jimmy swung it open and gulped. "Mr. Meyers." Had the man come about the box? Was Jimmy in trouble for taking it?

"Young man," he growled.

"I'm sorry, sir," Jimmy said, his gaze trained on his shoes. "I should have asked before I took the box."

"Never mind the box," the man grumbled. "Did you forget to deliver my paper to me today?"

Relieved the man wasn't mad about the box, Jimmy answered quickly, "No, sir. I took it right to your door."

"Well, it's not there," he grumbled, looking behind Jimmy at the Christmas tree across the room.

"Hi, Mr. Meyers," Laura Tremaine said. "Didn't the boys do a lovely job on the tree?"

Mr. Meyers's forehead crinkled. He didn't exactly answer, but gave a sort of grunt. Jimmy didn't know if it meant yes or no.

"I can show you right where I put it," Jimmy offered.

Before the man could answer, Jimmy took off for Mr. Meyers's house. He remembered putting it next to the welcome mat on the porch. It had to be there, unless someone had taken it.

But when Jimmy got there, it was gone.

He noticed, however, that there were pieces of pine tree and a trail of needles leading into the house.

Crouching down, he looked under a wrought-iron chair on the porch. Sure enough, the paper was under there. "Here it is," Jimmy announced as he retrieved the paper. "It must've been kicked under there when you brought in your Christmas tree."

"Well," Mr. Meyers took the paper, "I . . . um . . . thank you for finding it."

"You're welcome," Jimmy said cheerfully, anxious to get back to his family. He started walking away, then turned and said, "Merry Christmas, Mr. Meyers."

Back at home, Jimmy found his family even more excited.

"Guess what?" Charlie told him. "Mom's boss called and said they had some food left over and they're bringing it to us after the restaurant closes."

"Really?" Jimmy couldn't believe his ears. All they had in the house were a few eggs and some bread.

"They're bringing turkey and stuffing," Charlie said.

"And punkin pie," Lizzie added.

"Let's get the table set," Laura told her sons. "Then we'll be ready when the food comes."

As they put the dishes on the table, Jimmy asked his mom about Mr. Meyers.

"Why do you think he's so unhappy?" he asked. "He has money and a nice house and probably all the food and stuff he needs. Still, he's such a grouch."

"I know exactly why he's unhappy," Laura told her son. "He's lonely. All the money in the world won't give you love or keep you company when you're alone. I know we don't have much," she told all of her children, "but I have three sweet, precious children. You kids are worth more than any amount of money in the whole world."

"Mom," Jimmy said, after thinking about what she'd just said, "Do you think we could invite Mr. Meyers over to eat with us? You know, since he's all alone and everything?"

Laura looked at her son, then a broad smile grew on her face. "I think that's a great idea. Tell him we'll eat in about an hour."

Charlie and Jimmy both ran over to Mr. Meyers's house, but when they got there, he was gone. Full of disappointment, they decided to write him a note in case he came home in time to join them.

Gathering her children around her, Laura Tremaine read the account of the Savior's birth from the Bible.

Lizzie sat wide-eyed, listening as Laura told about the infant Jesus being born in a manger. "So, Jesus was poor, like us?" she asked.

Laura thought for a moment. "I guess He was."

"But He was a king," Lizzie said. "Even though we're poor, I can still be a princess, can't I, Mommy?"

"Yes, sweetie. You sure can," Laura said, giving her daughter a peck on the forehead. "Now, why don't we sing some Christmas songs?"

Lizzie's hand shot up. "Can we sing 'Away in a Manger'?" she begged. "It's my most favorite-ist Christmas song."

"Mine too," Laura told her daughter.

Together, they softly sang the sweet Christmas song, and as they sang the last verse, Jimmy felt a lump grow in his throat.

Be near me, Lord Jesus; I ask thee to stay
Close by me forever, and love me, I pray.
Bless all the dear children in they tender care,
And fit us for heaven to live with thee there.

There were tears in his eyes and a tingling warmth that spread throughout his body. Yes, his family didn't have much. They were poor, and they had to work very hard for everything they got, but Jimmy knew that Jesus was close by them. He helped Lizzie get better, and He blessed them that they would have a nice meal on Christmas Eve. Maybe there were other things they wanted and needed, but they were all together as a family. And that was something even money couldn't buy.

Suddenly, a knock came at the door.

"The food!" Charlie yelled as he flew to answer it. But when he opened the door, they were all surprised to see Mr. Meyers standing there with a large red sack flung over his shoulder.

"I got your invitation for dinner," he said, his voice still gravelly but not as grouchy as usual.

"We're so happy you could join us," Laura said warmly. "Come in. Let me take your coat."

He placed the red bag on the floor, and three pairs of eyes followed his movement with keen interest.

"On my way over, you kids would never guess who I ran into," Mr. Meyers said, gazing at the three eager faces staring up at him.

"Who, Mr. Meyers?" Lizzie asked impatiently. "Was it the men with our food?"

"No," he said. "It was this funny man with a white beard and a red suit."

Lizzie's mouth dropped open.

"And he asked me if I was heading to your house," he continued.

"And you said you were?" Lizzie was practically breathless.

"I did. And he asked me if I'd help him deliver these presents to you." He motioned to the bag. "He's got so many children to visit, he's worried he's not going to get all the presents delivered."

"You saw Santa? Cool!" Charlie said. His gaze darted to the window. "Is he gone?"

Mr. Meyers chuckled and nodded.

"Can we open the presents now?" Lizzie asked. "Please don't make us wait until morning, Mommy."

Mrs. Tremaine flashed a questioning glance to Mr. Meyers, who nodded his okay.

"Well, I guess while we're waiting for dinner to arrive, we might as well open the gifts."

Jimmy didn't know what to think as Mr. Meyers handed out gift after gift to each member of the family. He was even more amazed when each gift was opened. Charlie got a snowsuit, a warm hat, a football, a pair of jeans, and some nice warm snow boots.

"Alright," Charlie exclaimed. "No more duct tape."

Lizzie got a baby doll with a blanket, a china tea set, a necklace with a matching bracelet, and to her ultimate surprise and delight, a beautiful red velvet dress, with ribbons, lace, and a big bow that tied around her waist.

"Now I really am a princess," she said, holding the dress up to her. "And look, it has a little purse and a headband that matches." She twirled around to show everyone how beautiful the dress was.

Jimmy was thrilled with his hooded sweatshirt, baseball cap, new backpack with several reading books inside, and a thick, warm pair of gloves.

But best of all were his mother's gifts. One was a gift certificate to a clothing store in a shopping center nearby. She desperately needed a new coat and some shoes for work. Tears filled her eyes as she saw how much the certificate was worth.

"There's another box, Mommy," Lizzie said, handing her mother the last wrapped present.

"My goodness, I've got more than I deserve already," she said, resting her hand on her heart.

"Open it, Mom," Charlie said, full of wiggles and bounces of excitement.

Mrs. Tremaine glanced at Mr. Meyers, who gave her a nod to go ahead.

With some reluctance, she peeled away the paper and exposed a plain white box. When she lifted the lid, she gasped with surprise, her tears streaming down her face.

"It's just like the one John gave me," she said, picking up the figurine of Mary and running her finger over the glossy finish.

Mr. Meyers saw Jimmy looking at the figurines with open-mouthed shock. He gave the boy a knowing wink and half a smile.

Laura Tremaine looked at her children and added, "Yes, it's exactly the same—except this one's not broken."

All three of the children looked down at their shoes. Then Lizzie looked up, her own eyes filled with tears. "It was an accident, Mommy. I didn't mean to bump into the statues."

Laura held her arms out for her daughter, who rushed into her embrace. "I know, sweetheart. I know. Everything's okay now. Don't cry."

Lizzie sniffed and wiped her eyes on her shirtsleeve.

"Mr. Meyers, I don't know how to thank you," Mrs. Tremaine said to their neighbor.

"Don't thank me," he said, holding up his hands. "It was that Santa fellow. Thrust the bag right into my hands."

The doorbell rang, and to their delight, dinner was delivered. They received more food than needed and would have several meals of leftovers. Pumpkin pie had never tasted so good. And over dinner, the children asked Mr. Meyers question after question about his own childhood.

"What was Christmas like at your house, Mr. Meyers?" Lizzie asked.

"My family was very poor when I was young. I was born during the Depression, and my father did odd jobs around town to make money for our family. But it was never enough. Seemed like just as he'd get a little extra for Christmas presents and such, something would always break down or someone would get sick and we wouldn't have any money for gifts."

Jimmy felt like Mr. Meyers had described their lives exactly.

"It was hard being poor," Mr. Meyers said as he looked at the family in front of him. "But at least we had each other." His voice cracked as he spoke. He cleared his throat and said, "I'd give everything I own, every penny I have, to be with my family again."

"Where are they?" Charlie asked.

"Heaven," Mr. Meyers answered. "My wife and two daughters have all passed away."

Jimmy felt bad for their neighbor.

"I know you folks don't have a lot," he said. "But you have each other. That's the most important thing you could ever have."

Mrs. Tremaine smiled at the elderly man, whose face seemed to have softened in the short time that he'd been at their house. Jimmy noticed that the harsh lines around his eyes were more like friendly crinkles. His thin, stern mouth didn't seem as hard-set as it was before either. Had Mr. Meyers really changed, Jimmy wondered? Or had Jimmy just finally gotten to know the man better?

Charlie got up from the table and went to the cardboard Christmas tree and took down the star at the top. He brought it over and gave it to Mr. Meyers.

"Why, thank you, Charlie," Mr. Meyers said, admiring the glittering star.

"That star's the most special," Charlie explained, "because it's the one that led the shepherds and the wise men to Jesus."

Mr. Meyers blinked and nodded his thanks.

"Mommy, can Mr. Meyers come over for breakfast in the morning?" Lizzie asked.

"If he'd like to," Mrs. Tremaine answered her daughter. "That is, if he likes oatmeal."

Mr. Meyers pulled a face that made them all laugh.

"I don't want to see another bowl of mush in my life. That's all I ate as a kid. Tell you what," his eyes sparkling as he spoke, "why don't we go out for breakfast in the morning. My treat."

The kids exploded with excitement. "Can we, Mom?" they begged. "Please?"

Mr. Meyers looked at Mrs. Tremaine and said, "You'd be doing me a favor too," he said. "I'd enjoy having the company of your family. Besides, it wouldn't hurt to let someone wait on you for a change."

Mrs. Tremaine's expression reflected her thanks for the man's kindness. Jimmy liked seeing his mom happy. And he realized that even though on the outside Mr. Meyers seemed mean and crabby, he was a nice old man who was lonely.

"I'd better let you get your children to bed," Mr. Meyers said, grabbing his coat from the coatrack.

Mrs. Tremaine checked the clock. "Goodness, it is late. Lizzie, let's get you in the tub, then we can put some curlers in your hair."

"Can I wear my new dress to breakfast?" Lizzie asked.

Her mother nodded.

Lizzie shot out of her chair to head for the bathroom, then skidded to a stop, turned, and ran to Mr. Meyers, giving him a hug. "I'm so glad you're our friend," she said. "And if you run into Santa Claus, tell him that this is the best Christmas we've ever had." She took off for the bathroom again.

Mrs. Tremaine smiled and said, "I agree. Please tell him thanks for me too."

Charlie was next to hug Mr. Meyers. "I didn't say anything in front of Lizzie," Charlie secreted his words behind his hand, "but I wasn't so sure there really was a Santa. Until tonight. See you in the morning."

Charlie left to get dressed for bed.

Jimmy looked at his feet, not sure what to say. Thanks just didn't seem to be enough, but that was all he could come up with. "Thanks for getting us all these great presents and especially for getting my mom that nativity set."

"You're welcome, Jimmy. You know what?"

Jimmy shook his head.

"This is the first time in years that I've enjoyed Christmas. I haven't had anyone to buy presents for in a long, long time. You and your family helped me to have a Merry Christmas."

"I guess that's what Christmas is all about, isn't it, Mr. Meyers?"

"Yes, Jimmy. I guess it is."

About the Author

Michele grew up in St. George, Utah, and served a mission to Frankfurt, Germany. She and her husband are the proud parents of four children: Weston, Kendyl, Andrea, and Rachel.

Michele is the best-selling author of several books and a Christmas booklet, and she has also written children's stories for the *Friend* magazine. She enjoys corresponding with her readers who can write to her care of Covenant Communications, P.O. Box 416, American Fork, UT 84003-0416, or via email at info@covenant-lds.com.